Rob Astor

Leviathan

Rob Astor

Leviathan

JustFiction Edition

Impressum/Imprint (nur für Deutschland/only for Germany)
Bibliografische Information der Deutschen Nationalbibliothek: Die Deutsche Nationalbibliothek verzeichnet diese Publikation in der Deutschen Nationalbibliografie; detaillierte bibliografische Daten sind im Internet über http://dnb.d-nb.de abrufbar.
Alle in diesem Buch genannten Marken und Produktnamen unterliegen warenzeichen-, marken- oder patentrechtlichem Schutz bzw. sind Warenzeichen oder eingetragene Warenzeichen der jeweiligen Inhaber. Die Wiedergabe von Marken, Produktnamen, Gebrauchsnamen, Handelsnamen, Warenbezeichnungen u.s.w. in diesem Werk berechtigt auch ohne besondere Kennzeichnung nicht zu der Annahme, dass solche Namen im Sinne der Warenzeichen- und Markenschutzgesetzgebung als frei zu betrachten wären und daher von jedermann benutzt werden dürften.

Coverbild: www.ingimage.com

Verlag: JustFiction! Edition ist ein Imprint der
LAP LAMBERT Academic Publishing GmbH & Co. KG
Heinrich-Böcking-Str. 6-8, 66121 Saarbrücken, Deutschland
Telefon +49 681 37 20 310, Telefax +49 681 37 20 310-9
Email: info@justfiction-edition.com

Herstellung in Deutschland:
Schaltungsdienst Lange o.H.G., Berlin
Books on Demand GmbH, Norderstedt
Reha GmbH, Saarbrücken
Amazon Distribution GmbH, Leipzig
ISBN: 978-3-8454-4521-2

Imprint (only for USA, GB)
Bibliographic information published by the Deutsche Nationalbibliothek: The Deutsche Nationalbibliothek lists this publication in the Deutsche Nationalbibliografie; detailed bibliographic data are available in the Internet at http://dnb.d-nb.de.
Any brand names and product names mentioned in this book are subject to trademark, brand or patent protection and are trademarks or registered trademarks of their respective holders. The use of brand names, product names, common names, trade names, product descriptions etc. even without a particular marking in this works is in no way to be construed to mean that such names may be regarded as unrestricted in respect of trademark and brand protection legislation and could thus be used by anyone.

Cover image: www.ingimage.com

Publisher: JustFiction! Edition
is an imprint of the publishing house
LAP LAMBERT Academic Publishing GmbH & Co. KG
Heinrich-Böcking-Str. 6-8, 66121 Saarbrücken, Germany
Phone +49 681 37 20 310, Fax +49 681 37 20 310-9
Email: info@justfiction-edition.com

Printed in the U.S.A.
Printed in the U.K. by (see last page)
ISBN: 978-3-8454-4521-2

LEVIATHAN

By

Rob Astor

I'm flying! Arms spread, legs stretched, Evan floated through the center of the frigate's long super structure. He passed over metal walkways and under titanic bulkheads. At the far end, Evan held the palms of his hands out, gently pressing them against cold metal. Forward progression halted, Evan twisted slightly, easing down to the platform where his sneakers squeaked as they made purchase.

"Goofy kid," a figure to Evan's right said with a chuckle. Raven leaned against the wall, arms crossed over his wide chest. He wore a red flight uniform and white plasti-skin vest just like Evan's. They also had control pads wrapped around their forearms. "You never did waste time findin' a ship's 'sweet spot'." Raven wrapped an arm around his son's shoulders. He held Evan close, running his knuckles across Evan's skull, mussing an unruly shock of black hair with florescent pink streaks. "What's this? Get some new racin' stripes there, Small Fries?"

"Dad," Evan pulled back. "I'm almost sixteen."

"Medium Fries, then." Evan followed Raven down a set of metal stairs, walking back in the direction Evan flew from.

"We almost to Vega?"

"Yup. Should be finishing the jump in ten minutes. Get Scooper ready."

"Race ya!" Evan charged forward. "C'mon, old man, c'mon!" He grinned. "Let's see you bust one of those moves you're always talkin' about."

Raven flashed a grin of his own, rushing forward, easily catching the lanky Evan. His fingers found Evan's armpit, making the boy twist and laugh.

*　　　　*　　　　*

Seated at the navigation control, Raven Spade surveyed the debris ring of comets and asteroids surrounding the young blue star from a central holographic projection. Two additional holographic grids of yellow-orange hovered in the air before him. The one on Raven's left displayed an inventory list. On the right were detailed sensor readings taken from the frigate's position half a light-day from Vega. "Got Scooper on-line, Evan?" he called out.

Above and to Raven's right, Evan was seated at a control bank. "Almost," he said. Evan's fingers danced over holographic controls. He wore a headset with thin, transparent glasses, a box-like device and antenna on the right, and a second box on the left. Red lines of information scrolled past his eyes. Tapping a control, one line flashed. "Activated." Under the hulking mass of the frigate, hatches popped opened.

"Goin' in," Raven said. Chunks of rock and ice tumbled under the massive starship. Some of them neatly slid into the openings. Slight vibrations worked up through the deck plating where they were felt by Raven. He smiled. "I think we're gonna get a good haul today, buddy boy."

Evan smiled. He flipped a holographic control with the twist of his hand, pulling a second up with his other. "Melter's on. Refinery's on."

"Good work."

A light flashed on Evan's right. His brown eyes darted over. "We got company, Dad."

Raven's muscles tensed. "Marauders?"

"They're not in the habit of sending greetings before they attack," Evan said. "It's Jarrick Dane. He wants to dock."

"Let him in."

*　　　　*　　　　*

Compared to Raven's muscular form, Jarrick was pencil thin. He strolled down the ramp of his sleek blue delta winged Falcon carrying his flight helmet. The craft was neatly positioned at a diagonal angle in the bay, filling approximately a quarter of the space. "Don't tell me you came all the way out here to get a fresh drink of water," Raven said, pumping Jarrick's hand.

"Captain Dane," Evan said. He couldn't take his eyes off Jarrick's ears, almost perpendicular to his skull.

Jarrick grinned wide. "Evan Raptor! You get taller every time I see you." He rubbed Evan's head. "Don't you think it's 'bout time for a haircut? You know…" he ran his hand over his spiky black hair, "…a Marine cut like me?" Evan rolled his eyes as he fixed his hair. "What're you feedin' this boy?" he asked Raven.

"Everything the finest diners in F.F.P Space have to offer. So, why'd you come all the way to Vega?"

Jarrick's mood changed. "Got a lead on 'you know what'."

Raven's smile diminished. "Evan, get down to the Refinery. See if we picked up anything."

Evan sighed, slumping his shoulders. "Aye, dad." He walked slowly ahead, touching a button on the left side of his headset. Music filled Evan's ears. He reached the corridor and turned. In the shadows, Evan quickly pressed himself against the wall. Using his left forearm control pad, he lowered the volume.

"What'd you find out?" Raven asked, his voice a low rumble.

"The Marauders are looking for an alliance with the Eusian Empire."

*   *   *

Clothing covered in dirt and grime, Evan placed his headset next to the sink. Next, he took off his forearm controls and plasti-skin vest. Pulling off his sneakers, Evan dumped out black dirt. He didn't bother to undress further as he walked into the sonic showers. Evan pressed the activation button. Pulsing vibrations worked through his body, dislodging the filth from his clothes and skin, sucking it up into overhead vents.

"Evan Raptor Spade," a loud voice said, causing him to jump and spin simultaneously. His wide eyes landed on his grinning father.

"Goofy kid! No wonder the air filters have to be flushed so often."

Evan blew out a quick breath. "Better than fouling up the wash water."

"We get anything good?"

"Besides ice? A few thousand kilos of iron and some crystals."

Raven considered the information with a nod. "Not bad. Steak okay tonight?"

"Sure."

"When you're done, head down to Hydroponics and pick out some good vegetables."

"Dane staying?"

"No. He's out on business." Raven tapped the side of the door a few times and walked on.

*   *   *

Blinding white light pierced the vacuum. A matter stream shot straight at Mars. The stately, elongated silver-toned frigate jumped into real space.

On the bridge, Evan sat in the pilot's seat, keeping a close watch on holographic displays hovering around him. "Federation Of Free Planets Tracking has you on scope," a computerized female voice said. "Standby for transponder signal confirmation." Evan glanced up at his father seated at the Navigation Array. Raven smiled, flashing his son a thumbs-up.

"Frigate RS-149; transponder signal confirmed. Welcome to Mars, Raven Spade. You're cleared for docking at the Delta Spaceport Hub."

"Okay, Medium Fries, ease her in."

"Aye, dad."

Evan delicately throttled the ship toward the red and blue marble. Taking polar orbit, he flew low over the Borealis Ocean south to the mouth of Valles Marineris. A towering saucer-like structure hovered over an island like a black storm cloud, supported on huge stilts rising up from a metropolis situated below. Cutting back on speed, Evan eased into position as automated guidance systems took over the task of docking. "Good work, son," Raven said. "You'll have your Captain's License in no time."

Evan hopped out of the large seat as Raven began cycling down power. "Grab the cargo manifest."

"Got it. What're you forgetting?"

Pausing, Evan glanced around. He reached up and felt his headset, then his utility belt. "What's Captain Spade's first rule?" Raven hinted.

"Right!" Evan said. He reached back and pulled two flat chips from the main computer. They were crystalline rectangles with gold tips on each end. Raven repeated the rule with Evan. "Never leave without the Core Chips." Evan popped a hatch open on the back of his plasti-skin vest. Reaching over his shoulders, Evan tucked the chips deep into a neoprene lining and closed the slender compartment.

"Estimated time we're here?" Raven climbed backward down a set of steep stairs.

Tapping his left forearm control pad, Evan looked over a holographic list of cargo. "Eighteen hours max."

*   *   *

"Welcome to the 364th. Annual Martian Stellar Starship Show," the pleasant voice reached Evan as he and Raven walked into the city-sized geodesic dome housing hundreds of space ships.

"Whoa!" Evan gasped. He sucked on his strawberry-banana smoothie as they passed shiny red Racing Corvettes with graceful curves and sleek golden Speed Sliders. "Think they got any Federation ships on display?" Before Raven could answer, Evan saw something outside the dome, docked along the spaceport's rim. His jaw dropped. "Dad, look at that behemoth!" he pointed. "It's a Leviathan!"

The gargantuan craft was easily several kilometers long. A stunted nose formed the bridge and passenger area. Further back, huge circular compartments rotated around the length of the craft. It was so bulky and long, Evan couldn't see the engines. "Think of the fortune we could make hauling stuff with that," Evan commented.

"Leviathans are generational ships," a well-groomed young man with blonde hair in a black business suit said. He came over and offered a firm handshake to Raven and Evan. "Veddie Brock, United Federation Shipping."

"Raven Spade."

"Mr. Spade, what an honor and a pleasure to meet you sir. You've made quite a name for yourself. If you ever need extra work, be sure to come to my office."

"Much obliged."

"So, we can borrow your Leviathan, right?" Evan asked.

Veddie chuckled. He looked out at the mammoth bulk of the colossalus. "Unless your family's had one for the last few centuries, there's little chance of owning one, not to mention the cost when they do go up for sale." He grinned, turning back to Raven and Evan. "I hear it told even the Federation's bloated military budget couldn't cover the cost."

"Is that one for sale?" Evan asked.

"No. The owner's making a delivery. A big delivery."

"Try blutotanic. How long does it take to dump and pack?"

Veddie shrugged. "Depends on the size of the freight. This one's going to be here for the next three weeks."

*   *   *

"Casino Deck," Raven said as he and Evan stepped into the elevator. Someone touched a button. The elevator's doors closed. They rocketed up through a transparent tube.

"Dad," Evan sighed. "You know I'm too young to gamble." The Martian surface quickly retreated. Skyscraper and city lights blended into luminous cross-hatch art.

"Got a surprise for ya, Medium Fries."

Exiting the elevator, Raven walked past lines of slot machines straight over to the nearest bar. A huge holographic projection filled the wall, displaying news about recent Federation Navy activity. Raven stopped behind a hunched over man wearing a beat up brown leather coat with spiked brown hair and tapped his shoulder. The man turned, his angular face melting into a wide grin. "Raven Spade! Good to see you, my man." He stood, took Raven's hand and gave him a hearty slap to the shoulder.

"Uncle Gunnar!" Evan embraced the taller, broader figure. Gunnar worked his index fingers into Evan's armpits, unprotected by the plasti-skin vest, causing Evan to slip to his knees in a fit of giggles.

"Some things never change!" Gunnar said, pulling on Evan's right arm.

As Evan stood, Raven dug a card from his wallet and passed it to his son. "He's gonna make the next delivery with us. Go have some fun in the arcade for a few hours. Gunnar an' me's got some business to discuss."

"Aye, dad," Evan said happily trotting away.

Raven took a seat as Gunnar tapped a large coin loudly on the bar. "Two drafts."

"What do we know?" Raven asked in a low voice.

"We know who the Marauders' leader is. Someone called Bolton Archer."

"Really…"

"Name mean anything to you?"

The bartender set their beers down. Raven took a healthy swallow. "Federation drop out, 'bout twenty years back." Gunnar nodded lightly, his lips held in a tight line. "Didn't know he had the balls to lead a pack of pirates."

"Word is, Archer's skirting Eusian territory."

"Interesting… Dane says they want an alliance with 'em."

"That's bad enough to scare the ugly off a two dollar whore." Raven burst out laughing, patting Gunnar's shoulder. "Here's the kicker," Gunnar continued. "Archer's getting information from someone in the F.F.P."

"It just keeps gettin' better an' better, don't it?" Raven's eyes focused on the holographic news. A swarm of raiders in Swoop Jets dove around a fleet of bulky Federation Carriers. Armor piercing missiles pelted them with surgical precision. The slower turrets on the Carriers were no match for the smaller, infinitely more agile attackers. A line of shells neatly opened the side of one of the military dinosaurs, effectively crippling it.

"…the scene two days ago at 18 Scorpii when Marauders engaged F.F.P. Bulk Carriers. Caught completely by surprise, two were destroyed. The rest of the fleet was heavily damaged. The attack appears to be hit and run. Marauder ships immediately retreated from the area after the skirmish. No report is available on the number of casualties."

Raven shook his head and sighed deeply. A beeping sounded from his left forearm control. He touched a flashing red button. The stern holographic face of a man with white hair in his fifties materialized. "Admiral McMurrary. To what do I owe this pleasure?"

"I've got something for you, Spade." McMurrary's voice sounded gravelly. "A decommissioned Destroyer." Raven's eyes bulged. "I told you, I don't forget my allies. You'll find it at The Wheel."

*   *   *

Evan threw punches at his uncle, striking large red gloves covering Gunnar's palms. "C'mon, kid, really let me have it. Put all your strength into it." Evan thrust with all his might. Shifting on his feet, Evan circled Gunnar, grunts echoing in the empty cargo hold. "That's more like it. We'll make a man outta you yet!"

"What're you an' dad up to, Gunnar?" Evan asked, concentrating another series of blows on the red gloves.

"You shouldn't be listenin' in--"

"Don't give me any b.s." Evan planted three hard strikes to Gunnar's palms. "You've always been straight with me. Dane came all the way out to Vega just to talk. Twenty-six light-years is a pretty long way to make a social call." Two more hits squarely struck Gunnar's left palm.

"You know about the Marauders?"

"Who doesn't?" Evan finished his barrage.

Gunnar swallowed. "Okay, Evan, here it is. Your dad's a bounty hunter."

Evan snickered. "You're joking."

"He's working with the Federation to track down the Marauders' leader."

"Really?"

"You think that attack at Mu Ara was a random terrorist strike?"

Evan's face went pale. "I remember that day," he said softly. "We made some kinda top secret drop at the HR 6998 listening post and jumped over to Mu Ara Station Alpha."

*   *   *

Seated behind flight controls, Raven Spade eased his Frigate high over the space station's multi-tiered arcs. His dark eyes scanned passing traffic and available docking ports. Eleven year old Evan stood to Raven's right, chatting with a passing starship captain. "You can get a good price for iron ore from the Irams in HR 6094, and the best linguini this side of Italy."

"We'll keep that in mind," the voice on the com cheerfully replied.

"Goofy kid," Raven said.

"You always say to make friendly contacts, dad."

"At this rate you'll be the Federation's Goodwill Ambassador."

"There's a spot opening up," Evan pointed to the far end of the upper most arc.

"Okay, Evan. Here's how we take her in." Evan studied every move his father made. Minutes later, they connected to the station's docking clamps. Raven stood, walking toward the main computer bank. "Captain's rule number one. Never leave without the Core Chips. Everything we own is recorded on them. They're our identities and our money." He opened the back compartment of Evan's plasti-skin vest and put the crystal chips inside.

*　　　　　*　　　　　*

Holding the plastic glass high with both hands as he swallowed the last of his milkshake, Evan constantly swung his legs back and forth under the table. When he set it down, he wiped his lips with the back of his right hand. "Need anything else there, partner?" Raven asked, taking a bite of steak.

Evan leaned back in his seat, right hand placed on his stomach. "I'm good." His legs continued to kick.

"Hmm. Thought I was gonna have to get a second job just to pay our dinner tabs."

Dressed in a full body green robe to compliment his aquamarine scales, the waiter paused at their table. "Will there be anything else?" he asked, voice deep and ragged, sea green eyes darting between father and son.

"I think we're all set," Raven said.

"Very good, sir." He reached for Evan's empty glass. The sleeve pulled up, revealing a series of numbers branded under his yellowish forearm.

"Hey, Mister, what's that?" Evan asked, pointing at the waiter's arm.

Yellow flushed the waiter's cheeks. His eyes misted. "Federation scum," he snapped. Evan's legs stopped kicking.

Raven quickly turned to the waiter, taking his arm. "Hold on there a minute, pal. He's just a boy. He doesn't know anything about those markings."

The waiter took several quick breaths through his nose and pulled his arm free. "Then why don't you tell him?" He briskly walked away.

"Sorry, dad," Evan said softly. His feet pedaled lightly at the air.

"It's not your fault."

"Why'd he get so mad?"

"I really don't know, son. Eusians never need a reason to be mad at us. Just seems like they always are."

*   *   *

Back on the Frigate's bridge, com-chatter filled the semi-darkness. "Oops. I forgot to cut off the radio, dad. Sorry." Evan began activating various holographic displays.

"Don't sweat it. We got solar panels. I wouldn't want you missing' out on all the gossip, now would I?" Raven tussled Evan's shaggy black hair. Raven took the Core Chips from Evan's plasti-skin vest and made his way back to the main computer.

"Mayday! Mayday!" a voice yelled loudly through the com speaker. "We're under attack! Somebody, help us!"

Evan rushed to the forward view port. His heart pounded in his chest. Several small Swoop Jets plowed their way through traffic. "Shields," he yelled. Fiery explosions rattled the station, shaking the Frigate loose from its docking clamps. Evan fell to his side.

"Rotate to starboard, ninety degrees!" Raven said, leaping into the pilot's seat. The Swoop Jets fired rockets at the bridge. On his knees, Evan ducked, hands over his head. The raiders sailed overhead and to their right. The missiles proved ineffective, spinning harmlessly away. More cries for help sounded through the radio. "Shut that off. Send out the distress signal and turn on the Jammer."

"Aye, dad."

Raven pulled his freighter around just as the Swoop Jets tumbled back for another pass. "Rail guns on-line." A second volley of missiles streaked towards them. Raven pressed a holographic control, unleashing a steady stream of 200mm pellets. The projectiles exploded well out of range while three of the Swoop Jets crumbled into useless piles of scrap metal. Evan cheered, his arms held high over his head.

Clearing the length of the Frigate, the Swoop Jets jumped out of the system. "Looks like they're gone, dad."

"What's the situation outside?"

Evan pulled up holographic scans at a terminal to the left of the forward view. "Lots of escape pods. A ton of smashed up ships. Station Alpha's calling for Federation back-up."

"Okay. Let's get the tractor beam on-line and pull some of those people in."

*　　　　　*　　　　　*

"When the Marines discharged your dad, he did delivery runs. Winning a few tangles with some pretty tough pirates and Eusian Border Patrols got the Federation to secretly re-commission him. They sent him out to find the pirate's main base and put an end to their organization. He'd been chasing leads for years. Someone at the listening post set your dad up that day," Gunnar told Evan. "He was supposed to be killed. We just learned it had to be a Federation Officer." Gunnar paced, taking a few breaths.

"The Feds wanna kill dad?"

"No, just one person. Or a small group. Someone who wants the pirating activity to continue."

"Why?"

"To keep attention off the Eusians."

"What've they got to do with it?"

Gunnar shrugged. "No one knows for sure. Could be expansion plans. Or, they might have something to hide."

"Something the pirating activity would help cover up."

"Yeah. They could very well be in league with the Marauders."

*　　　　　*　　　　　*

The glassy pin wheel-like construction of the spaceport rotated high over the green and blue planet Marineau gave the station its well known nick name; The Wheel. Two yellow suns hung high in the sky while a third smaller red star rested just above the horizon. The triple system created prismatic reflections in the floating disk as it rolled on its side in relation to the planet's surface. Air traffic was heavy. Ships of all shapes and sizes hovered close.

"Welcome to Alpha Centauri," Raven Spade said with a wide smile, shifting into the automated docking signal. They pulled up next to a Federation Destroyer. It was an intimidating sight to behold. Re-enforced armor plating. High speed gun turrets. Bridge tower stacked like a bulky skyscraper. "There's my new lady," Raven grinned.

"I like to keep my sex organic," Gunnar said. "You just know some fine Marineau is gonna rock my world tonight." He and Evan began switching equipment off.

"Don't forget to pack your bags, Raptor," Raven tapped Evan's shoulder. "That ship out there's our new home."

"Had 'em ready before the last drop." Evan took the Core Chips from the main computer and worked them into the rubbery lining in the back of his plasti-skin vest. "You got my ticket, right?"

"Right here." Raven placed a plastic card in his son's hand.

"You didn't get one for me?" Gunnar did his best to sound offended. "I see how you are."

"Go on, you." Raven gave him shove.

*   *   *

Evan walked up behind Raven and Gunnar. He wore black leather pants, a silky silver colored button down shirt, a black leather tie, and his white sneakers. Evan jumped up on his uncle, gaining a piggy-back ride. "Get everything to our rooms?" Raven asked. They circled the space station's perimeter on a platform housing bars and restaurants.

"Yep."

"I see you clean up pretty good, too."

Evan lowered himself, walking between the two larger men. "So what're you guys doin' tonight?"

"Takin' yer old man out to have some fun for a change," Gunnar said. He stopped in front of blacked out windows. Thumping sounds emanated from behind them. Neon Marineau lettering flashed over the door. Gunnar pulled it open. The trio entered a black light environment. Percussion driven music vibrated their breast bones. Heavy smoke filled the air. Loud voices, cheering, and shadowed bodies contributed to momentary confusion. Evan's white sneakers, silver shirt, and pink highlights glowed.

On a stage at the center of the club, a two meter tall Marineau female performed a pole dance. Her skin was spotted blue and pink. A tuft of frizzy blue hair ran down the center of her skull to her neck and back. Fish-like fins served as ears. Long black eyelashes batted at several male patrons. She puckered large pink lips at the end of a stunted, snout-like face. A long, slender tongue flicked out of her mouth. Her arms were wrapped around the pole as she slid down between two rows of four breasts, spreading her legs wide while whipping her furry tail in lazy circles.

"Oh, wow!" Evan gasped, mouth gaping.

"Eyeballs back in your head, goofy kid," Raven said, holding his hand over Evan's face. Evan pulled his dad's hand down, finding his vision quickly blocked a second time. "You better get to your concert. No photo ops here." Gaining a third peek, Evan was led to the door by Raven who blocked his eyes over and over. "Don't get into trouble tonight."

"Aye, dad," Evan said. He kept dodging his dad's hand as Raven opened the door and shoved him out. Gunnar laughed while Raven shook his head. The door opened. Evan stepped back in.

Raven glanced back, doing a double-take. "Get goin'!" He raised his arm to shoo his son away. Evan quickly exited.

Joining Gunnar, Raven took a seat at a table to the left of the stage. "You ready for this?" Gunnar asked.

"Ready as I'm ever gonna be."

"What about Evan?"

"He's been followin' in my footsteps since before he could walk. Besides, you'll be lookin' out for him. Just stick to the plan."

*   *   *

The black claw-like Eusian Pincer slid into orbit high above Marineau. Half a dozen Swoop Jets flanked it.

"You're sure Spade's there?" the pilot asked. His wiry frame was draped in a black leather trench coat. Long, stringy brown hair covered the right half of his face. A black metal patch was riveted over his right eye socket.

"Information came straight from the top, Archer."

The left corner of Bolton's mouth turned slightly up. *I can't wait to get my hands on that Destroyer.* "We're about to become very wealthy, boys." With a few Eusian modifications, *I'll be overlord of any planet I choose.*

*   *   *

The lift transport was crowded. So many people. So many species. Most were wealthy Marineau dressed in flowing toga-like gowns. Ondurokir, with their boney heads, shoulders, and backs, wore the least amount of clothing. Essentially, just a pair of pants. A small group of Eusians in full body green robes clustered to the far side, staying near humanoid species Evan wasn't familiar with. Most humans he saw wore flight suits. A few were dressed in brightly printed shorts and shirts. They descended toward a sprawling city, the lift clearing the tops of buildings three kilometers tall.

"So, you come around here much?" a female voice asked.

Evan turned. She was taller than Evan. Slender with long curly brown hair, creamy complexion, deep blue eyes, and red pillow lips. She wore a red sweater, black leather skirt, and black high heeled boots. Evan's cheeks burned. His breathing quickened. He stammered. "Hey. No. Just staying a few days while my dad gets a new ship."

"Cool. So, you're a Spacer."

"It's really just a glorified name for a delivery boy." They both laughed.

"My name's Tash." She held out her right hand. "Tash Bertina Randolph. Cute hair, by the way."

Evan blushed. "Thanks. Evan," he took her hand. "Evan Raptor Spade."

Tash's eyes lit up. "Any chance you're related to the hero Raven Spade?"

"Yeah, he's my dad."

Tash leaned on folded arms on the lift railing. "You checkin' out the Speedy Neophytes concert tonight."

"Yep." Evan patted his pocket. "Got my ticket right here."

"We should hang out," Tash smiled. Evan's jaw dropped. "Don't get any cute ideas. I'm not one of those girls who picks up every Spacer boy who comes to town!" They both laughed again.

The lift settled into a magnetic dock. Passengers began debarking, filing along a polished garnet plaza with neatly spaced palm trees and a large central fountain. Ahead of Evan and Tash was the group of Eusians. Once their feet touched the pavement, the pair walked toward a circular crystal stadium. "Any idea what's up with the Eusians?" Evan asked. "I've never seen so many this deep in Federation Space."

"There's some important dignitary here. The Eusian Matriarch sent him to address the Marineau Commonwealth." Tash suddenly smiled wide, pulling Evan by his arm.

"Hey."

She jogged up to a stand surrounded by a myriad of other people. Tash looked down at Evan with a playful gleam. "Since I'm going to show you around, the least you can do is buy me a hot dog."

"We haven't seen anything yet," Evan laughed.

Tash put on a fake pouty face. "I'd hate to have to twist that cute little arm right out of its socket." She grinned. "Just ask my last boyfriend how painful it is."

"What do get on yours?"

"Everything."

"Of course."

Tash poked his side. Evan's arm blocked defensively.

*   *   *

"I think you'll find the weapons compliment we left installed more than adequate," Admiral McMurrary's holographic projection said. "Unfortunately, we couldn't leave it all behind. Some of it was Classified.

Your defensive systems have been upgraded. You've got enemy weapon scrambling capabilities and extra layers of shielding. If that's not enough, we tripled the hull plating."

Raven examined lists generated from another display across the bridge. "Everything looks good on this end, Admiral." He faced the white haired Federation Naval Officer. "We never discussed terms of payment."

"Take out those pirates. They've caused too much damage."

"Count on it."

"Your transponder signal will still read as military issue, however, there's an embedded code to give you free access to all Federation star systems. You won't get any flack about registration."

"I appreciate that."

"Good luck, Raven Spade." Admiral McMurrary offered a stiff salute. Raven returned it.

When the Admiral's image faded, Raven brought up multiple holographic lists. "Disable the following weapons systems," he said and began touching holographic buttons. "Scramble access codes. Encrypt with sixty-four million layers." The computer system beeped.

"Establish a covert communications link with the ship at these coordinates." Raven used an index finger to pull up a holographic panel. A detailed chart of the Orion Nebula popped into view. Inside one of the squares was a ship. Raven touched it. A Leviathan diagram enlarged to fill the frame. He punched in sets of numbers. "Keep this link open at all times. Make sure no diagnostic tests reveal it under any circumstances. It is first priority for back-up power systems. Access can only be changed by Raven Spade. Scramble and encrypt with sixty-four million layers." The computer system beeped a second time.

*   *   *

Pulsing lasers accompanied sixty-fourth and one hundred twenty-eighth keyboard notes, creating a sonic double helix as sound swept across the auditorium. Driving rhythm pounded a steady undercurrent while galloping electric guitars howled counterpoint melodies. Near the stage, Evan and Tash danced, their bodies pressed against other gyrating kids. Some hovered in groups to the far left and right.

Evan took Tash's hand and motioned with his thumb. At the side, Evan grinned and jumped up, using his feet to push away from the side. He performed a series of low gravity flips. Tash's eyes grew wide. Her expression hinted she was impressed. Evan motioned for her to try.

Tash leaped at the padded wall, pushing with her feet back toward Evan. He held her hand, guiding her through a series of complex twists. "Incredible!" she yelled over the music. "Where'd you learn to do that?"

"No different than finding a ship's sweet spot," Evan said loudly. He leaped at the wall, bounced back and flew over to the other side of the stage where he pushed himself back to Tash.

*   *   *

Tash stopped before the dimly lit front door surrounded with potted trees and shrubs. The sounds of crickets filled the quiet evening. "I had a really great time, Evan," she said.

"Me, too," he smiled.

"Thanks for the t-shirt and holo-vids."

Evan shrugged. "My dad's loaded. Besides, you didn't give me much of a choice. I like my arms attached to my body."

Tash bent down. She gave Evan a kiss on the cheek and a long warm hug. "Hanging out with you today was almost like having a little brother." She stood straight. "Next time you happen to be in town, be sure to call." She handed him a scrap of paper.

Evan's eyes twinkled. He grinned. "I will."

Tash opened the door, waving. "See ya." The door closed.

What a great night! Evan bounced along the sidewalk back to the hovercab in Tash's driveway. "Spaceport lift, please," he said, crawling in.

*   *   *

Under the glare of the plaza lights, Evan stepped up onto the transport lift. High up in the sky above the city, The Wheel slowly spun, a cosmic gem against the backdrop of stars. Pastel lights illuminated every curved, wedge-shaped section. Scores of ships buzzed around the colorful spaceport, visible because of red and white flashing lights. Larger ships looked more like fuzzy globules, dwarfed by The Wheel's immense bulk.

Evan leaned his back against the side railing. A group of Eusians clamored aboard. Their traditional green robes had blue sashes adorned with an assortment of medals and ribbons. Wonder if it's that dignitary and his entourage Tash told me about.

A shorter Eusian balanced himself on a tall wooden scepter, his steps coming much more slowly than those around him. His robes were brushed velvet. The back had a train of fine blue feathers. On his head, the Eusian wore a tall hat woven from some form of leafy vegetation Evan didn't recognize.

The dignitary saw Evan watching him and offered a kindly smile and nod. Evan returned the smile. He turned sideways in relation to Evan, the yellowish underside of his forearm exposed, revealing a set of branded numbers on his scales. Evan thought back to the time he first saw those of the waiter at Mu Ara.

The last of the Eusians shuffled aboard. The lift attendant closed the metal gate and touched a glowing yellow button on the control pad. Evan felt his stomach sink as they rose up into the night air.

*   *   *

Without its running lights on, the charcoal colored Eusian Pincer was invisible. Spinning down through the atmosphere, it was tailed by the Swoop Jets.

"Time to collect, boys," Bolton Archer said. "Group One, attack the Frigate. Group Two, secure that Federation warship. I'll meet you there."

"Acknowledged."

*   *   *

A blinding flash of red light caught Raven's attention. An expanding plasma cloud thumped against the Frigate's port hull, rattling the length of the ship. The fiery mass contracted on itself, pulling back superheated gases, sucking debris into a micro-singularity and taking a fairly large chunk of the ship with it. A nearby shuttle was swept into the fray, instantly breaking apart and vanishing. Within the span of a few seconds, the singularity vanished.

"So that's what it is," Raven said softly. A second singularity snapped the frigate neatly into two sections. The bow ripped itself free of its moorings and lazily plunged downward. Several smaller ships were crushed under the massive hammer.

Raven fell backward through a circular opening, landing upside down in a huge leather seat. Quickly, he slammed a hatch closed and punched buttons. Another series of explosions sounded. Raven pulled down on a handle.

Three black holes formed under the falling section of the Frigate. The hull explosively fragmented. Twisted, red-hot metal fragments zipped into the singularities. In an instant, the Frigate disintegrated and vanished, the trio of black holes sealing themselves.

*   *   *

Everyone snapped their heads skyward at the sound of the first explosion. "Get down! Get down!" the lift attendant ordered. He dropped into a sitting position against the side rails, holding his arms over his head. Metal fragments whizzed past them.

A brighter flash illuminated the scene so Evan could see the Frigate was under attack. "Oh no! Dad!" He scrambled over to the lift operator. "Hey, you gotta make this thing go faster!"

Something large and black bounced off the lift. Evan fell to the floor while most of the Eusians slipped over the guard rail. "Help!" The dignitary was near the side, sliding uncontrolled toward a long fall.

Evan scrambled over and grabbed his arms just as the Eusian's legs dropped over the edge. Quickly, Evan jammed his feet against one of the railing's metal bars. The fall was halted, but the Eusian's weight pulled hard on Evan. "Hold on," Evan said, barely able to breathe as he strained. He squeezed his hands as tightly as he could to maintain a firm grip on the elder man. "Whatever you do, don't let go!" Evan pulled back as hard as he could, his back against the deck. He took in as much air as he could every second.

Evan gazed up, just in time to see the bow of the Frigate vanish from sight. The underside of The Wheel loomed close. Twenty or thirty seconds more! He had to hold on!

The muscles in Evan's arms screamed. His knuckles hurt. His legs and feet cramped. Perspiration beaded on his forehead. Evan's hands sweated. Scaly skin slipped slowly under his fingers. More deep breaths. His abdominal muscles burned. Almost there!

The transport platform locked into place. "Help! Help!" Evan yelled. The lift operator jumped off and ran. Numerous others passed by without so mach as a glance; strong Ondurokir, lean Marineau; all more capable of hoisting the Eusian up than Evan was. He gulped air. Can't hold much longer! "Somebody! Please!" Salty fluid stung his eyes.

A familiar yet confused face appeared in the crowds. "Uncle Gunnar! Uncle Gunnar!" Evan's legs vibrated from strain. Gunnar's head snapped around, searching for Evan. "Here! Over here! Help us! You gotta help us!" Gunnar spotted his nephew and jumped onto the platform. "Hurry! I can't hold on!" Evan hyperventilated between grunts.

Gunnar braced against the railing, grabbing the dignitary's arms. "Hang on! I gotcha!" Groaning, he pulled the Eusian to safety.

Panting hard, Evan released his grip, arms and fingers wracked with pain. "Oh god… Oh god…" he trembled. The elder statesman lay on his back, breathing as hard as Evan.

Gunnar embraced Evan. "You okay?" Evan nodded.

*   *   *

The Eusian Pincer sat down in the main landing bay of the Federation Destroyer next to three Swoop Jets. Glaring white lights made the Pincer's obsidian surface blacker still. The claw ship's main hatch opened. Bolton Archer stepped out. He pulled leather gloves off, slapping them in his right palm. Archer surveyed the interior of his capture.

A pilot in a black flight suit and helmet saluted him. "The Wheel's signaling for Federation assistance, sir."

"We better get moving."

On the bridge, Bolton sat in the Captain's chair. His men took posts at other stations. "Power up." He leaned toward a terminal. "Let's see what you're made of." His index finger touched a button and lifted a holographic panel. He scrolled through the weapons inventory. "Well, Spade, looks like your Federation friends didn't trust you with anything more than civilian armaments."

Pulling up another hologram, Bolton frowned deeply. He fired the main engines. The entire spaceport vibrated. "Break us loose, boys."

Massive gun turrets rotated, popping shells into the docking platform. Metal explosively sheered away in wild lotus blossoms of orange. The Destroyer floated free, blasting additional shells into the back half of Raven Spade's Frigate. Its remaining bulk shifted into the station, upsetting The Wheel's axial tilt. The squared nose of the massive Destroyer plowed into smaller ships waiting to dock, charging into the upper atmosphere.

"Send a priority signal coded Top Brass," Bolton said. "Audio only."

"We're through."

"Raven Spade's been dispatched. I've got the Destroyer. We're headed to Rendezvous Point Gamma. Awaiting further instructions. End transmission." Archer tuned to his crew. "Good work men. Now let's jump outta here."

In front of the Federation warship, a brilliant lightning-like matter stream lanced through the night sky, plunging a needle deep through folded space. The titanic ship instantly lunged forward, vanishing through a pinpoint aimed at infinity.

*   *   *

Elbows propped on his legs, Evan sat on the plush white davenport in the Eusian dignitary's brightly illuminated suite. Skylights allowed for maximum use of visible energy from the three suns of Alpha Centauri. Evan wore his standard red flight suit, white plasti-skin vest, and forearm control pads. His headset encircled his skull. The glasses did nothing to hide his bloodshot eyes.

A glass coffee table rested before Evan. He listlessly scrolled through holographic news reports via a control pad on the edge. The attack on The Wheel last night was exclusive news on every channel.

"…of this magnitude makes it the single most blatant Marauder assault in the history of the Federation Of Free Planets," one middle aged man was saying. "Planet Marineau has never suffered terrorism since joining the Federation two and a half centuries ago. The target, the popular spaceport known as The Wheel. It suffered considerable damage. A civilian Frigate owned by courier, and Spacer hero, Raven Spade was also destroyed. In the midst of the chaos, a Federation Destroyer was stolen and managed to escape before help could arrive."

Evan sat back and folded his arms over his chest. "Casualties ran high. Several civilian ships were damaged in the carnage. At least two dozen dock workers were killed. Eusian Viceroy Wexam lost half the members of his Viceroyalty Entourage. And, it's believed Raven Spade himself was also killed. The nature of the weapons used during the attack is unknown. F.F.P. spokespersons have declined any comments until a complete analysis--"

Evan cut the signal as the suite doors opened. Gunnar sat next to him, presenting him with a foam box. "Here's some breakfast, Medium Fries."

"I'm not hungry." Evan's chest tightened. "I can't believe dad's gone." He wiped a tear from his right eye. Gunnar placed an arm around Evan's shoulder.

Viceroy Wexam entered from an adjoining room, followed by Eusian staff members and Federation Officers. He was dressed in full dignitary regalia, holding a new wooden scepter. "Gentlemen," Wexam said. His aged voice was soft and raspy.

Gunnar stood, bowing. "Viceroy."

"Allow me to introduce Lieutenant General Kolt of the F.F.P. Marine Division." Kolt was tall and lanky with short blonde hair and a hollow face. He wore a standard gray Federation uniform.

"Pleased to meet you," Gunnar shook his hand.

"I'm serving as Admiral McMurrary's envoy. He sends his apologies and regrets he was unable to join us in person."

Wexam sat in a chair near Evan. The others took seats around the glass table. The Viceroy's speech was slow, hampered by quick breaths between almost every word. "Let me begin by saying that the Eusian Matriarch will be most anxious to hear of developments regarding this senseless act of violence. I am most certain, considering the grievous loss of life, she will open talks of entering into an alliance with the Federation to meet the mutual goal of putting an end to these so-called Marauders."

"Viceroy, at this point in time, the Federation Of Free Planets would welcome any help directed at stopping this menace," Kolt said. He looked at

Gunnar. "Admiral McMurrary wants you to continue Raven Spade's work since you were so closely involved."

"We got anything more to go on?"

"Tell him of the preliminary reports, Lieutenant General," Wexam said.

"Scans captured by The Wheel's sensor net have revealed some intriguing information. The weapons that destroyed the Frigate weren't standard issue by any means." Kolt swallowed hard and glanced briefly at the Viceroy. "In fact, the weapons are Eusian technology."

All human eyes looked to Wexam. The Viceroy held out his hand. His eyes closed. "Let me assure you, the Matriarch has no intention of going to war with the Federation. Someone stole the technology from us. They have been trying to incite a war by attacking outposts along our borders for the last fifteen Federation years."

"Me an' Raven were led to believe the Eusians attacked first," Gunnar said.

"That has only been true in isolated instances."

"What kind of weapons were used?" Gunnar asked Kolt.

"The Federation doesn't know how they work. What we do know is… perplexing. Sub space all around the area was punctured. Somehow, a plasma detonation created a micro-singularity."

"A what?"

"A tiny black hole," Evan said softly.

Gunnar stared at Wexam. "I am no scientist, young man. I cannot explain how they work either. I only know their power is enhanced with a special diamond. Which reminds me…" Wexam dug under his robe, pulling up several golden chains. From one of them hung a red diamond octahedron pendant. Taking the necklace off, Wexam held it out to Evan. "I didn't get the chance to properly thank you for saving my life last night. You're a very brave boy and you have my deepest gratitude."

Evan's eyes sparkled as he looked at the diamond. His mouth hung open as words failed him. "Th-Thank you." He put the gemstone on, tucking it under his plasti-skin vest.

"The properties of these diamonds are highly unusual. They focus the plasma in some way. That is how these singularities are created. Of course, this makes them very valuable. To my knowledge, they are only mined in ancient asteroid swarms."

"And, it's looking as if the Marauders are holed up in one," Kolt said. "I can transfer all the intelligence to you. Will you be staying here on Marineau?"

"No, we're headed to Tau Ceti," Gunnar said.

"Ah yes, planet Ondurok," Wexam mused.

"Contact Admiral McMurrary when you get there." Gunnar nodded. Kolt and his men stood. "Viceroy."

"Thank you for being here this morning, Lieutenant General."

The Federation Officers exited the suite. Evan looked at Wexam's aged face. "Viceroy. May I ask you something?"

Wexam smiled. "You kept me alive. I will talk to you about anything you wish."

"Those numbers on your arm…" Wexam's face paled to a yellowish hue. "I saw them once before, on another Eusian. He got mad when I asked what they were. Will you tell me?"

Wexam lowered his head, sighing deeply. He raised himself up and smiled. "Truly wonderful are the innocent," he said to Gunnar. Then he smiled at Evan. "Always full of curiosity." The Viceroy pulled his sleeve completely up. "I am afraid what I have to say is a very bad bedtime story. These numbers… They are used for identification purposes. In places where it is convenient for no one to remember your name."

Wexam stood, leaning on his scepter. He walked over to the window. "There is a great suffering, and an even greater injustice being inflicted upon my people. In the last two decades, millions of Eusians along the border territories have been captured and enslaved." Evan and Gunnar exchanged nervous glances. "I was one of them once. Taken from my home during a night raid. Stashed inside the cargo hold of a livestock transport. That's what we called them, you see. We weren't shown kindness or extended any dignities. We were animals. And treated as such."

The Viceroy turned from his window, making his way over behind the davenport where Evan and Gunnar sat. "All of us went through processing centers. They stole our lives, but, they didn't take our names. No. They branded us with hot steel, leaving these marks on us. These," he clenched his fist, "these were our new names. Now we were their property."

Slowly, Wexam paced. "I was taken to an asteroid mining camp. We dug eighteen hours every day searching for those precious red diamonds. Blood diamonds they call them, because of their color. Fitting description considering how many have perished. There was little food or water. We fought over scraps. So many injuries. So much sickness. Slaves dropped where they worked, the life going right out of them. Eventually, they took us to a hospital. At least, that is what they called it. It was located in the star system we call Blaiku. In the old tongue, Blaiku means 'destruction'. It wasn't a hospital, of course. No. It was a great big freezer. Many of my friends died there, calling out for mercy until their voices got too weak from the cold. The Butcher of Blaiku slaughtered thousands upon thousands of nameless Eusians. I waited for my end. I dreaded every day my eyes opened. I forgot what it was like to live without constant fear over my shoulder. You see, there was no hope. We all knew we were going to die. It was just a matter of time."

Taking a breath, the Viceroy eased himself back into his chair. "One day, a ship showed up. Some of us overpowered the crew. We escaped."

"You were the lucky ones," Evan said.

"No." Wexam lowered his head, shaking it. "The fortunate were those who perished."

"I… I don't understand."

He smiled at Evan. "Age has a way of making you look at life differently, my boy. You will understand. In time. I am not so lucky, as you say. No. I carry the memories inside of me every day I draw breath." The Viceroy tapped his chest. "I carry deep regret that I was unable to help any of the others who were left behind." His hand rested over his heart.

"That gives me more incentive to stop those pirate bastards," Gunnar growled.

"Pirates?" Wexam said. "You misunderstand me, young man."

"Viceroy?"

"I was not talking about pirates." Wexam raised an index finger. "There are some things my government does not want to come to light just yet. This is one of them. It is feared the Federation will twist this information around and use it as an excuse for pre-emptive strikes against us."

"Why would the Federation consider that?" Gunnar asked.

"That man, the Butcher of Blaiku, he is a Federation named Bolton Archer."

Evan's face paled. Gunnar's blood ran cold.

"There are those of us who want to shut those camps down when we can find them. But, we cannot risk war with the Federation."

"Archer's head of The Marauders."

"Not twenty year years ago," Wexam said. "And even to this day, he is working with someone within the Federation. This we know. We do not know who." The Viceroy folded his scaly hands and brought his index fingers up to his lips. "The Eusian Matriarch does not wish to bring dishonor to the whole F.F.P. No. She is wise enough to understand that all of your people are not aware of this atrocity; this plight of ours. It is not the fault of the people for these rogue actions of military miscreants. She just wants to put an end to the madness."

"Count us in," Gunnar said.

*   *   *

Bags strapped over his back, Gunnar looked up at the docking platform numbers and checked a plastic card in his left hand. "Yep. This is it." He turned to Evan, setting his bags near the boarding ramp of their shuttle transport. Evan stopped next to the railing, setting his bags down, rubbing his right shoulder. Gunnar looked at his watch. "Still got a few minutes. You want anything to eat or drink before we go?"

"No, I'm okay."

"Evan? Evan?" He and Gunnar looked at nearby passengers. "Evan!" Tash came jogging up. She looked different wearing jeans and a sweatshirt with her long hair in a pony tail. Tash gave Evan a quick hug. "I'm so glad I found you before you left."

"How did you find us?" Gunnar asked.

"My mom asked the Port Authority." She glanced over to the side. A short woman with long brown hair wearing a light blue skirt and blazer smiled at them. She held her hand up in greeting.

Gunnar smiled and nodded. "Evan, I'm gonna go over and say hello."

"I heard the news about your dad," Tash said. Her eyes clouded. Tash's voice caught in her throat. "I'm so sorry."

Evan managed a nod, looking down at the metal walkway.

Tash wiped a tear from her eyes. "Listen…" She swallowed hard. "I didn't come down here to get all mushy on you and stuff. My mom wanted to ask you guys to stay with us."

"Uncle Gunnar and me got some work to do for the Feds."

Tash nodded. "Well, be careful." Evan nodded. She bounced on her heels. "You think you'll come back this way soon?"

Evan shrugged. "Never know in this business. I still got your number."

"And you better use it," Tash waggled her index finger at him. "If I find out you passed through and didn't come by to say hi, I'd have to pull all your limbs outta their sockets." They laughed again and embraced.

*   *   *

The woman smiled as Gunnar approached. "Hi, Gunnar. It's been way too long."

"Lillian," Gunnar smiled. "It's good to see you."

"You know you're welcome to stay here with us."

"Duty calls."

"But, it's so dangerous for a boy Evan's age." Gunnar nodded. "Being a Spacer is a really tough life. He could stay and get a proper education."

"Raven always wanted me to care for Evan, you know that." Lillian nodded, folding her hands in front of her. "Besides, this whole mess will be taken care of soon enough," Gunnar said.

"It's all I can do to keep a straight face in front of Tash."

"She doesn't know about--"

"She knows a few things." Lillian glanced over at her daughter. "She's keeping up a strong front, too." Lillian gazed into Gunnar's eyes. "It would kill me if anything happened to Evan. Promise me you'll keep him safe."

Gunnar nodded slightly. "You have my word. And don't worry. We'll get together real soon. Take care." He patted Lillian's arm. Lillian smiled, her gaze drifting over to Evan.

*   *   *

Yellow and orange suns hung high in the sky, baking parched land. The azure was devoid of clouds, as arid as the sand below. Artificial globe-like structures of limestone and glass sat on the outskirts of a large city capped with a dome of diamond-shaped panels of glass and crystal. Basking in the sun, Eusians relaxed naked on rectangular rocks. Some sipped tall drinks and rubbed oils into their scales.

Jagged white lightning slashed across the wide open blue. The huge, blocky rectangle of a Federation Destroyer loomed into view, casting a dark shadow over the resort. Eusians stood, gawking at the mammoth ship.

A wall of sand rushed toward the area, propelled by a loud blast of sound. It rolled through, an unstoppable shockwave tossing transports and other loose vehicles through the air in a whirlwind. Glass windows shattered in the wake of the wave. People struck by it went tumbling through the air. The ground below the leading edge of the Destroyer was scoured, swept clean.

Swoop Jets dipped out of the Destroyer's main hanger, twisting and turning erratically toward the city. Missiles punched holes in the main dome, granting the raiders passage. Rail gun fire from the Destroyer quickly tore apart the protective shell.

Fiery explosions ripped through the heart of hexagonal city blocks. Eusians ran, ducking for cover under large stone overhangs. Globe buildings exploded in fantastic flashes of orange. Fiery glass and stone fragments rained down like napalm on everything.

The leading edge of the destroyer plowed through the opening in the main city dome. Like a bullet passing through an eggshell, the warship wasn't to be stopped. Lumbering to the city's center, breaking thrusters fired, shattering any remaining glass. Cargo transports dropped out of the main hanger, settling down on streets and in parks.

Bolton Archer exited the first transport, holding a machine gun in each hand. He was followed by a squad of his men, dressed in standard gray Federation uniforms. Bolton fired rounds into the air as he strolled up to a group of cowering Eusians. "Get in that ship, you filthy lizard maggots!" he said. He shot at the ground around them. They ran for cover under another stone overhang. Bolton shot a few of the nearest Eusians. Metallic squealing escaped writhing bodies. "I hate repeating myself. Now, get in that ship!" He fired the guns again. "Let's move it! Haul ass! Haul ass!"

Holding hands over their heads or clutching the nearest live body for support, the Eusians half-walked, half-stumbled over to the transport. Ripped green robes were splattered with bloody blue ooze. "Get in there! Go on! Get inside! We got diamonds to mine." Archer's men zapped the Eusians with electric cattle prods, herding them up the ramp. Some yelped in pain. Others squealed.

*   *   *

Viceroy Wexam shuffled into the Eusian Matriarch's receiving area, the tip of his scepter punctuating each step with a soft click. His Viceroyal Staff was in tow. The regal Eusian Matriarch sat on a throne of blue and green marble covered with green throw pillows and draped needle point linens. Its wide stone base was flanked by a contingent of guards holding long spears with axe-like lances at the tips.

The Eusian Matriarch's attire made the Viceroy's robes look cheap. The royal robes were woven from blue and green velvet and silk, sporting a cape fashioned from incredibly large dark blue feathers. The leaves on her headdress were three times as large, fanning out like the branches of a tree. Emerald stones hung in a chain around her neck with a baseball sized emerald cut azure diamond resting between her breasts. Her folded fingers were adorned with precious green and blue stones at every knuckle.

Pausing at the foot of the throne, Wexam bowed deeply, keeping a firm grip on his wooden scepter. "Most majestic Eusian Matriarch," he said.

She smiled softly. "Rise, my dear, dear friend." Her blue eyes sparkled. Green facial scales had a bluish tinge to them. "It is most unfortunate, the level of Marauder activity in days of late. Another of our fringe systems was attacked. As many as thirty-five thousand Eusians are either dead or missing." Wexam's head lowered, slowly shaking from side-to-side. "You spoke with a Federation representative about our willingness to eradicate the pirates?"

"Yes, your grace."

"I think we should add a little temptation of our own to this plot." The Eusian Matriarch slowly stood, gently pacing across the highly polished blue marble floor. "I wonder how fast we could draw these criminals out into the open if they were made aware of Project Dreadnaught."

"Most majestic, would that be wise? Project Dreadnaught is our greatest achievement. I shudder to think of the consequences if it were to fall into the wrong hands. The Marauders would be virtually unstoppable."

The Eusian Matriarch smiled. "We will not hand it over to them as a present. No. However, we can bait a trap."

"Most majestic grace, we have a plan in motion with Federation Operatives. Admiral McMurrary has Raven Spade's brother and son working for him."

"Very good, Viceroy. What I'm proposing is, offer a key piece of technology to them. Technology irresistible to the Marauders. Then, we let out just enough information about Project Dreadnaught…" The blue left her cheeks as her mouth curved down and her kindly expression turned sour. "…To draw them into the open…" She curled her fist. "…And crush them."

*   *   *

Gunnar hopped out of the transport first, setting his bags to the side. He reached back, hefting Evan down to the dirt concourse. "Ever been planet side before, buddy?" he asked.

"No."

Gunnar pointed at the marshlands beyond the landing area perimeter. "Those are the Ceremonial Mounds of Ondurok. Locals go there to pray for favors." He picked up his bags and walked toward the main gates.

"Who do they pray to?"

"Toppor. See the river?" Evan nodded. "That's Toppor River. It always flows in the direction of Toppor." Gunnar pointed at the brassy yellow gas planet hovering in the sky forty-five degrees east of the orange star Tau Ceti. "The locals believe he's the father of their culture passed into the divine state."

"Maybe we should go pray with them," Evan said.

"Why's that?"

"It'll take a miracle for us to help the Eusians." They exited the terminal and walked down a gravel path toward turtle shell-like humanoid dwellings built of wood and stone sprinkled near the spaceport.

*   *   *

Inside his spacious garage, Gunnar pulled an old parachute tarp off a bronze colored Racing Corvette. Evan's eyes bulged. His jaw dropped. "Awesome!" Evan checked the underside near the engines. "It's a classic!" He looked at his uncle. "Why didn't you tell me you had one of these? I could've been flying it."

"Suddenly, I remember why I didn't say anything. You ain't got your pilot's license."

Evan inspected every inch of the engines. "Dad let me fly the Frigate."

"In wide open space."

Evan hopped up on the side to peek into the cockpit. "I know how to dock, too."

Gunnar picked up an old rag. "Hey, hey! Do you mind? Footprints."

"Sorry." Evan kicked off his sneakers. He wrapped his hands around his face as he tried to see the controls.

Gunnar rolled his eyes. "Goofy kid." He began wiping dust off the curved hull. "Your dad and I were gonna surprise you with this when you turn twenty. He's been sending me spare parts whenever he found things at the shipyards."

"Really?" Evan's face was a broad smile. He slid in his socks to the edge and jumped down onto Gunnar, arms and legs wrapped tightly around him. "This is the best present ever." Gunnar patted his back, waiting for Evan to let go. "You know you're my favorite uncle, right?"

"I'm your only uncle." He held his arms out, still waiting for Evan to let go.

"Then we agree you're my favorite."

Gunnar placed his index fingers in Evan's armpits. Instantly, Evan laughed and let go, dropping down to the floor. "You could be a torture risk, you know." Grinning, he helped Evan back up to his feet. "C'mon. Let's get 'er flight ready."

*   *   *

Turning a ratchet inside a cast iron block, Gunnar's attention was torn between his work and the holographic news from the tool bench terminal. Much like the Marineau incident, the new attack was getting the entire Federation's media coverage. Admiral McMurrary stood aboard the bridge of a Federation ship, talking to a young reporter with patchy brown and orange skin. Triangular shaped spikes surrounded her head.

"…spokesperson for the Eusian Matriarch said this was the single largest attack on their sovereignty in twenty years," she said. "Does it trouble you a Federation Destroyer was used in this attack?"

"I'm greatly disturbed," McMurrary said. The lines in his face ran deep. "The Federation doesn't attack without provocation."

"Sounds like he's another lyin' windbag based on what the Viceroy told us," Evan grumbled. He was on his back under the Corvette, wearing his red outfit minus his sneakers. His feet were planted on the floor, knees up against the flaring side. Evan twisted a ratchet of his own, removing a panel.

"Makes me wonder if we should trust him." Gunnar used a rubber hammer to gently tap apart sections of metal. Where he scratched an itch on his forehead and nose, Gunnar's fingers left greasy smears.

"Does the Federation know who's responsible for the destruction at HR 7162?"

"Not conclusively. The Destroyer was recently decommissioned." McMurrary chose words carefully.

"Here it comes," Gunnar said softly.

"The ship was registered to Raven Spade. Since there's no direct evidence he was killed at The Wheel, Spade or any number of his affiliates could have--"

"What?" Evan said loudly. He pulled himself from under the Corvette's hull and sprang up. "What did that bastard say about my dad?"

"Take it easy, sport," Gunnar said, holding Evan back from the holographic projection.

"Nobody can survive a singularity, you stunted old geezer," Evan directed to the Admiral's projection.

"The F.F.P.'s gotta lay the blame on someone. Can't tarnish their brass, you know. Best thing we can do is get the 'Vette up and runnin' so we can get on with clearin' your dad's name."

Staring at the Admiral's hologram, Evan heard Gunnar's words. His eyes slowly drifted up to his uncle. "You're right." Evan's body relaxed. "Let's get crackin'."

*   *   *

"I'm beat," Evan said. He was slouched over, eyes half-closed, arms wrapped around his legs.

"Don't give up on me now." Gunnar yawned loudly. He was under the Corvette's engines. He blinked his eyes several times and twisted his face around. "We're almost done."

"You said that four hours ago." Evan lay his head on his knees. His eyes closed.

"You took a nap six hours ago and missed all the excitement. The Marauders hit a Federation Border Patrol at 31 Aquila. Got their asses kicked this time." Gunnar tossed a grease rag at his nephew. "Found out their not so bad without their Destroyer backin' 'em up. You even missed Kolt's call sendin' us the Federation Intel."

"Uh-uh." Everything faded from Evan's perceptions. He slipped down a long black tunnel. Overlapping images filled his brain for an unknown length of time. Evan's muscles reflexively tightened when cold water shocked his system. With a huge gasp, Evan was standing, dripping wet. Gunnar grinned at him, holding an empty plastic bucket. "All done."

"Ever hear of alarm clocks?" Shivering, Evan looked at the Corvette. The shiny hull looked brand new. "It's beautiful," he whispered. "You're gonna let me fly it first, right?" Evan grinned at Gunnar.

"Let's get cleaned up." Gunnar's hair was matted with oil. His face smeared with grease. His clothing covered with dirt. Evan didn't look any better.

They went into a small room at the side of the garage where the sonic showers were. Gunnar touched the activation button and peeled of his shirt. Evan walked right in with his clothes on, letting the pulsing vibrations shake his body and break away the filth. "No wonder your dad had to get the air filters cleaned all the time," Gunnar said.

"You sound just like him."

"Goofy kid."

*   *   *

High above the limb of the Earth, the yellow sun sparkled brilliantly off the Pacific Ocean. From the surface of the continents, slender shafts six hundred kilometers tall poked through Earth's atmosphere and connected to an artificial ring system encircling the equator. From the position of the Federation Cruiser, Earth's moon was positioned behind the planet. The night side of both bodies and the metallic ring glowed with campfire-like lights.

At the side of the main view port Evan leaned against the bulkhead, arms folded over his plasti-skin chest, his right foot pressed up against the frame under his butt. Gunnar paced in front of him. "As strict as the military is, you'd think an Admiral could keep an appointment," he said.

"I wonder what's so important we had to come like yesterday." Evan scrolled through data in his headset lenses.

"Beats me, kid," Gunnar shrugged.

"Don't know why I gotta be here."

"Partners. Remember?" Evan rolled his eyes. He dropped his foot.

Admiral McMurrary and Lieutenant General Kolt stopped next to them. "Gentlemen," McMurrary said. Because of his gravelly voice, he sounded more gruff than intended.

"Admiral," Gunnar nodded.

"That was some harsh b.s. you were sayin' about my father," Evan said. Gunnar's eyes almost popped out. McMurray stiffened.

"Easy there, tiger," Gunnar whispered in Evan's ear.

The Admiral cleared his throat. "We recovered sensitive Eusian technology after that skirmish at 31 Aquila. I want you to test it for us."

"What kind of technology?" Gunnar asked.

"A cloaking device."

Gunnar stared at the Admiral and then at Kolt. "Okay," he nodded.

"It's a simple test," Kolt said. "Our engineers wired it up to a Speed Slider. Fly out, engage the cloaking device, and go down to the Canne Band."

"Why do we gotta go to Earth?"

"Veddie Brock of United Federation Shipping has something that was smuggled out of the Eusian Empire by one of our spies," McMurrary said. "Pick it up. Engage the cloak. Jump over to Fomalhaut and back. I'm sure I don't have to tell you what a boon a cloaking device would be to Federation forces."

*   *   *

"Try to keep the tip of your nose level with any horizon references, like the docking bay floor," Gunnar said. He sat behind Evan. "Okay, ease 'er out."

Evan's hands were wrapped around the black wheel with only two side grips. A series of button panels rested just below the central shaft. He pushed the column gently forward. The long orange nose of the Slider knifed into the ebony of space.

"Good boy. Now, engage the cloak."

Evan found the switch on the panel and flipped it down. "You think we're just sensor invisible, or totally invisible?"

"Readings back here say it's a scattering field. I think we're sight unseen."

Evan grinned. He pushed the wheel forward. The slider lunged, jetting away from the Federation Cruiser. "Hey, Raptor, I said take it easy!" Spinning, Evan dove under freighters and sailed around shuttles.

*   *   *

Balancing on one leg to get the second free, Gunnar held his hand against a platform support beam. "How many years you tryin' to take off my life?" he asked.

Evan chuckled. They walked across the wing to the rear fuselage and climbed down a ladder to the ground. "I'm surprised this model even comes with an escape pod."

"Never know when those'll come in handy with all the pirate activity in the universe."

They exited the docking area and entered a large greeting center. "Welcome to the Canne Band Docking Information Center," a pleasant sounding computerized female voice said. The interior walls were white. Large holographic displays were spaced apart every few meters.

"Now, let's find Veddie's office," Gunnar said.

*   *   *

The corporate headquarters echelon of the artificial ring system resided in the central area of the Canne Band, fifty levels away from where the Slider was parked. Evan looked through plate glass windows into every office they walked past. Frosted white letters announced who was located where.

Gunnar and Evan walked into receptionist's area of the United Federation Shipping office. A young woman sat behind a glass desk, typing information into a blue holographic display. "Welcome to United Federation Shipping. May I help you?"

"Admiral McMurrary sent us to pick up a package," Gunnar said.

"One moment, please." She touched an intercom button. "Mr. Brock, Mr. Spade is here for Admiral McMurrary's delivery."

"Send them in."

"Go through the door behind me please."

"Thanks."

Gunnar and Evan walked toward the white panel. It slid aside. Beyond was a spacious office decorated with finely polished wood furnishings cushioned with black leather. Veddie Brock sat behind a desk large enough to be a cafeteria table. Behind him was a large view port where the blue and green of Earth was visible so far below. "Gentlemen, welcome," Veddie said. He was smiling, his fingertips forming a pyramid before his chest. He glanced at Evan. "So, you're Raven Spade's son."

"Yeah."

"I remember talking to you about a Leviathan not long ago."

"You must have a pretty good memory."

"You need one to succeed in the shipping business. Besides, who could forget your wild hair." Evan chuckled, remembering his bright pink highlights. "Please, have a seat." Gunnar and Evan sat in chairs in front of the desk. Veddie pulled a metal case from under his desk and set it before Gunnar. "Here's your cargo."

"Thanks," Gunnar said.

"You know, Raven Spade made quite a name for himself being a Spacer. If you two ever want a steady job doing deliveries, be sure to come back and see me."

"Thank you, sir. We'll keep it mind."

*   *   *

Starlight spun around the Slider as it trailed the lightning-like discharge through folded space. Dazzling Fomalhaut jumped into view. The star was shrouded with a ring of debris. Wide lanes were carved out where planets swept material clear near their orbits.

Evan was seated behind Gunnar, studying holographic readouts. A yellow-orange light flashed. The circle surrounding a diagram of the Slider disappeared. "Uncle Gunnar, we got a problem."

"What's up?"

"Cloak's off-line." A second hologram popped up, flashing a sensor warning. "Now we're being scanned."

"Great. How long before we can jump?"

Evan checked another readout. "Five minutes at least."

"Couldn't the F.F.P afford a Jump Maximizer?"

"Worry about it later. We got company." The holographic screen showed seven ships closing in.

"How're we set for weapons?"

With his index finger, Evan quickly pulled up a list. A short list. "Dozen rockets. Few thousand rounds of mini-rail gun pellets. Two hundred medium range turret caps."

"Looks like we're gonna have to dance."

"Six Swoop Jets and a Eusian Pincer coming in at ten o'clock."

"Marauders." Gunnar turned the Slider over, swinging up and around the pirates, escaping the first round of fire. "Shoot some rockets!"

Evan targeted one of the Swoop Jets and launched two missiles. The first swung too wide. The second clipped the starboard wing, ripping it apart in a flash of red. Gunnar fired the rail gun. The outer hull of another Jet fragmented, leaving a trail of debris behind the wounded craft.

"The Pincer's signaling us," Evan said. "Audio only."

"It might buy us some time. Let's hear what he has to say."

"Game's over Spade," Bolton Archer's voice filled the cockpit. "Surrender now and we won't leave you out here to freeze."

"Shove off, traitor."

"Hey, I thought you were gonna buy time."

A blinding yellow energy discharge streaked past the starboard wing. "What the hell was that?"

Evan pulled up the Slider's exterior sensor readings. "Polaron burst."

"He's got a Polaron Cannon?" A second blast tore into the left wing. Evan yelped in fear. The Slider jerked to the right, spinning wildly. "Sorry, Medium Fries, time to bail. Activate distress beacon." Gunnar pulled on a release lever to the left of his seat. He and Evan slid backward and down into the escape pod. A hatch slammed shut. The pod was jettisoned like a rifle bullet out the back of the Slider.

*   *   *

Archer smiled as the Slider's wing exploded, sending the small fighter into an uncontrolled roll. "Tractor 'em in, boys."

"The escape pod was launched."

"Get it." *Wouldn't want you to miss the party.*

*   *   *

Free floating in the open void, Gunnar and Evan's spacesuits were tethered together with a long belt. "This has got to be the lamest idea in the whole history of lame ideas!" Evan said.

"It bought us that time I was talking about." The metal case intended for Admiral McMurrary was duct taped around Gunnar's chest.

"The minute they open that tin can and don't find us, they'll be back out here with a search party."

"I don't plan on staying very long. The distress signal was coded for the Feds." Gunnar spotted a ship jumping into the system, a bulky brick-like Federation Gunboat. "In fact, here comes our ride now."

For several minutes, the ship remained stationary. Eventually, it dipped toward them, looming up like a giant sea creature. A tractor beam tugged on them, reeling them into a small shuttle bay. The hanger's hatch closed. A hissing sound faded into hearing range as breathable air was pumped inside.

Gunnar popped his helmet open. "Let's go see the commander." Evan unsnapped his helmet and adjusted his headset.

Just as Gunnar reached the entrance, the door slid up revealing a squad of men in Federation gray training handguns on them. Evan's eyes bulged. "Bolton Archer is most anxious to talk to you, Spade." Swallowing hard, Gunnar raised his hands.

*   *   *

Evan paced in circles, bending his knees repeatedly. "Evan, park it," Gunnar said, seated on the bench against the wall. "You're only making me more nervous." He wasn't in his space suit and the metal case was gone.

"I can't help it. I gotta pee. Really bad."

"Didn't your dad ever tell you to go before you left?"

"That was at Tau Ceti."

The door slid open. Two soldiers grabbed Evan's arms and pulled him into the corridor. Gunnar was on his feet, charging for the door. "Hey! Take it easy!" Gunnar snapped. A gun was forced into Gunnar's ribs.

"Archer wants to see the two of you."

They walked down a long metal corridor and exited the Gunboat by stepping onto a lift. It was parked inside an enormous rocky cavern. Swoop Jets and the Eusian Pincer sat near the far end. Evan tried to ignore the burning sensation down below. He bounced on his knees to a lesser degree, gazing around the inside of the chamber.

As the lift contacted the ground, Evan was shoved forward. Two soldiers held Gunner back, twisting his arms behind him, pushing him forcibly forward.

Bolton Archer walked up to them, meeting Gunnar's glare. "So, you're the legendary Raven Spade's brother. Pretty devious trick you pulled out there, leaving that escape pod empty." Then he looked at Evan. "I wanna talk to you first. Take Spade to Sparky." His gaze never left Evan.

Gunnar struggled, wrenching his body around. "Don't you hurt him, you son of a bitch! You hear me? I'll kill you!" Two additional soldiers helped subdue Gunnar and drag him away.

"Think you were goin' to a costume party, did ya?" Archer asked, pulling at Evan's hair. He removed Evan's headset. "You won't be needing that anymore." Bolton dropped it, grinding it underfoot. "Or those," he said, pulling the latches loose on Evan's forearm controls, sliding them off. "Check him over, boys."

Strong hands suddenly worked up and down Evan's legs. Fingers probed deeply into his pants pockets. "Wh-what do you want?" Evan asked. The back compartment of his plasti-skin vest was opened. "Nobody undresses me on the first date."

"Smart ass."

Hands rubbed Evan's back briefly. The vest hatch was closed. "Let's take a walk, boys."

"Where're we goin'?" Evan asked.

"Let's go see Cook, shall we?" Archer flashed an evil leer. "Maybe get something to eat. You hungry?"

"Can I go to the bathroom first?"

*   *   *

Four men wrestled Gunnar through the doorway. He jerked his torso sideways and kicked. One landed a blow to Gunnar's stomach. It didn't slow his efforts. Several more gut punches had no effect. Another punched Gunnar square in the jaw, disorienting him. They slammed Gunnar backward into a metal chair and strapped his arms down with metal brackets. Another encircled his stomach. Then his lower legs and skull.

Winded from the struggle, one of the soldiers said, "Sit tight. Archer will be back soon." The veins in Gunnar's arms stood out as he tried to pull his wrists free.

*   *   *

Evan squeezed back his urine so hard, his pelvic muscles hurt. He was led into a large kitchen area. To the right were a bank of grills. To the left, racks of dishes. Beyond them were deep tub-like sinks, some filled with stacks of dirty plates, others filled with water. There was a freezer to the back.

Pausing at the center of the room, Archer stood in front of Evan. He pulled a butcher knife from one of the racks and turned it over and over in his palm. Evan's breathing quickened. His heart hammered against his ribs. Sweat beaded on his forehead. "You want to be a good boy, don't you Evan?" Archer asked, rubbing the boy's black and pink hair.

Shaking, Evan nodded. "Y-yes," his voice trembled weakly.

Archer thrust the knife up to Evan's throat, holding the blade against the jugular. Evan's eyes closed. "What?"

"Yes," Evan said slightly louder.

"Good." Archer withdrew the knife. "I don't like having to repeat myself. You remember that and we'll get along just fine."

Evan opened his eyes. "Okay."

"Let's talk about money." Archer picked an apple from one of the plates on a rack and sliced it in half. He took a bite, smacking his lips. "Your father must've made a fortune. But my contacts can't find any account records." Evan's face burned as he remembered the Core Chips. "Now, I want you to think about this long and hard for a bit, Evan. I want to know where your father's money is." Archer took another bite from the apple, holding the knife up against his left shoulder. His eyebrows raised. "Take all the time you need."

"I-I… don't know."

Archer swallowed. He made a sound in his throat. Bolton moved in close and brought the knife down to Evan's abdomen. He unleashed a powerful jab with his right fist, plowing up into Evan's stomach. The air rushed out of Evan's body. He fell to his knees, the inside of his pants getting dark and wet. For long moments, he couldn't draw in a breath. When his body let air back in, Evan gasped deeply, moaning with every exhalation.

Setting the knife aside, Archer took a handful of Evan's hair and pulled the teenager up. "I thought you wanted to be a good boy."

"We… we…" Evan struggled to talk. "The computer wasn't… the file transfer. It wasn't done… when you attacked."

Taking Evan by the back of the neck, Archer pulled him over to the grill and forced his head down close to the hot metal surface. Evan screamed, his hands seeking anything to give him leverage. He couldn't push up against the larger man. He cried out with every breath, his cheek getting hot.

Without warning, Evan flew backward, sprawled across the floor near the sinks. Archer glared at him, his face a mask of rage. "Cool him off!"

Several hands clasped around Evan's limbs. Before Evan had any idea what was going to happen, he was plunged down into one of the water filled sinks. They forced down on his chest as he tried to pull himself up by gripping the side. Evan hadn't got a breath and clenched his teeth tight. Straining, his face turned red. Water burned his nasal passages. Swallowing pulled burning water down his throat.

Evan was yanked up. He coughed, sucking in a breath as he was thrust back down. Beating hard inside his brain, Evan's heart raced. The combined strength of the soldiers easily kept him in place. Evan beat his arms on the metal sides and wiggled his body, trying to slosh the water down far enough so he could breathe. Any efforts to escape only made it more difficult to keep holding his breath. Evan's lungs heaved to induce respiratory movement. Water trickled down his throat.

Lifted again, Evan panted heavily, coughing up water. He twisted to the side in an effort to crawl out. They pushed him down a third time. "No! No!" He frantically contorted his body. Evan took in as much air as he could. A solid hand at the back of his neck plowed his face into the metal bottom. His arms were pinned this time, held behind his back by his captors. He couldn't even pull the plug on the drain. There was nothing Evan could do now except wait.

Evan anxiously tried to think of anything to distract himself from his desperate physical need for air. The beating of his heart grew loud. It felt like it was pounding against a vice. All too soon, Evan's lungs burned as hot as a blast furnace. Muscles quivered. His diaphragm was on fire. Water found its way up his nose. Clenching his mouth tight, Evan squeezed his eyes shut. His chest cavity heaved repeatedly. Precious bubbles escaped from between his teeth. Unable to stop the inevitable, Evan made sounds in the back of his throat, trying to plead for his life. His throat tightened, holding back water. Seconds later, in one loud burst, Evan lost his breath, causing a state of mental delirium as tense muscles relaxed. His entire perception was fuzzy and whirling.

The next thing Evan knew, he was being dragged along a corridor behind Archer. Head spinning, Evan was too weak to try and escape. He was thrown headlong into a holding cell. Hurting and breathing hard, Evan remained on the floor.

*   *   *

Storming into the command center, Bolton grabbed the metal case and sat at the main computer. *Raven cost me a fortune. I'll get my money's worth. Out of his worthless little brat in the diamond mines.* He flipped the lid, revealing a Eusian computer. Archer attached cables from the main computer to slots in the Eusian device and called up a holographic file directory. The word Dreadnaught caught his attention.

"Dreadnaught?" He touched the word, bringing up the schematic of a Eusian warship. "Well what do we have here?" He grinned.

Dreadnaught was shaped like a flattened falcon's beak with reptilian-shaped quadranium hull plating from stem to stern. At seven kilometers in length, it was one and a half times the length of a standard Leviathan. The more Archer read, the wider his smile grew.

*   *   *

To Gunnar, it felt like hours elapsed since being strapped into the hard metal chair. His efforts to escape renewed as soon as Archer came through the door. "You're not going anywhere, hotshot. Now you're a permanent guest at my labor camp. I'll find some little asteroid for you and that twerp kid to rot away in. This system's full of 'em."

"What'd you do to him?" Gunnar growled.

"Washed him up a little. You know, I can't believe he and Raven didn't even have the good sense to save the Frigate's Core Chips." Gunnar stared at Archer, trying to discern what he was after.

Bolton tapped a control on the wall. A holographic display of the chair and power level controls appeared. "Let's you an' me talk about the Eusians."

"About how many you've enslaved and killed?"

Archer's face hardened. He used a finger tip to activate the power and then raise it up. Gunnar thrashed around in the chair Gurgling sounds escaped his throat. Bolton turned the current off.

Breathing hard, Gunnar collected himself and glared at his captor. "You'll have to do better 'an that."

Bolton boosted the power up half way to maximum. Gunnar had no control of his limbs or the sounds escaping his mouth. Hot needles jabbed into every nerve. The electrical burning stopped, but, Gunnar's entire body vibrated, every muscle pulling against every other one.

"Let me give you some advice, Spade. I don't like repeating myself. I get very angry when I have to keep asking the same questions over and over. Do you understand?" Gunnar nodded, face glistening with sweat. His breathing was ragged. "Good. Think long and hard about this. Take all the time you need. I'm in no hurry." Archer smiled. He positioned himself behind Gunnar and leaned down to his right ear. "Tell me what you know about the Eusian Dreadnaught." Gunnar's eyes closed.

*   *   *

Evan's clothes were still damp when he woke. He pushed himself off the floor with his hands and stood, stretching. Muscles he never knew existed hurt. He sat on the bench, rubbing the back of his neck.

The door opened. Gunner was flung in. He took long, uncoordinated steps and fell over, twitching. Evan rushed down to him. "Uncle Gunnar." He grasped Gunnar's bicep. Gunnar pulled it back, scooting over to the wall. "Uncle Gunnar, it's me. Evan."

Gunnar stared at him a few seconds. "Evan," he whispered. "You okay?"

"I'll live." Evan took his arm.

Gunnar braced against the wall as he tried to steady himself. He leaned over on Evan, arms wrapping around him. "You're all wet. What's the matter? Wearing your clothes in the sonic shower isn't enough anymore?" Gunnar stumbled over to the bench and rubbed his face. "The labor camps. They're here."

"What?"

"Yeah. All over this system. Archer told me."

There was an explosion. The whole room shook violently. Evan fell on top of Gunnar on the floor. Klaxon alarms sounded. There were footsteps outside, trampling down the corridor.

"What's goin' on?" Evan asked. Distant gunshots echoed. Gunnar stood, bracing against the wall. Another explosion rattled the room. The power flickered. Smoke poured in from a ventilation shaft. Evan coughed. He beat his fists on the door. "Help! Somebody, help!"

The door slid open. A soldier took Evan by the arms. "Where are you taking us?"

"Admiral McMurrary decided to mount a rescue mission when you guys never returned," he said. A second soldier braced Gunnar from under his arm. They moved as quickly as they could down the corridor.

*　　　　　*　　　　　*

"Thanks for coming after us, Admiral," Gunnar said as he and Evan walked toward their Racing Corvette in the Federation Cruiser's docking bay. "I'm sorry they got the cloaking device and the spy package. You got a traitor in your midst. I'm sure we were set up. Keep your eyes open."

"We're sweeping the area for Marauders. We'll know who the informant is soon. Did Archer say anything about the package?"

"Yeah. He wanted to know about a Eusian Dreadnaught."

McMurrary rubbed his chin. "Dreadnaught… Ominous sounding name. Given the advanced state of Eusian technology, it can't mean anything good. I'll call in re-enforcements. Whatever a Dreadnaught is, we can't afford The Marauders getting their hands on it."

"Call in some humanitarian aid, too," Gunnar said. "This whole system's a great big labor camp. There's an unknown number of Eusian prisoners out there bein' used as slaves to mine the asteroids."

Admiral McMurrary nodded. "We'll send a transmission to Viceroy Wexam."

*　　　　　*　　　　　*

Ghostly white cloud formations awaited Gunnar and Evan as the Racing Corvette jumped into M42. "What're we doin' way out here in the Orion Nebula?" Evan asked. "I thought we were goin' back to Tau Ceti."

"Got a surprise for ya," Gunnar said. He flew through pillars of gas, following a particularly knotted strand up to a point where, one day, a star would emerge. Drifting in orbit around the stellar cloud, Evan spotted a Leviathan.

"Don't tell me you were holding one of those out on me, too." Gunnar smirked.

*　　　　　*　　　　　*

"Welcome to the bridge," Gunnar said when he and Evan exited the turbo lift.

"Blutotanic," Evan whispered, looking all around.

"It's got everything. Scramblers, Jammers, Modified Scanners, and a Jump Maximizer."

"How in the world can you afford one, Uncle Gunnar?"

"He can't," someone in the shadows said. Evan spun around. The voice sounded familiar. Raven Spade walked into the open. Evan's jaw dropped. "But, we can."

"Dad." Evan rushed up to Raven, embracing him tightly.

"Miss me, Raptor?"

"You're not dead! You're really here." Evan looked up at him. "How? What…?"

"It was all part of the plan."

"Plan? What plan? Why didn't anyone tell me about it?"

Raven sat at the nearest control station. "A plan set in motion to destroy The Marauders. It's taken a lot of time and effort."

"Did you know, Gunnar?" Evan pivoted to his uncle, his face blank. Gunnar didn't say anything. He folded his arms and stared at the deck. "You knew. You knew." Evan's voice cracked. "You kept it from me." His throat quivered. "You let me think dad was dead? Why did you let me think dad was dead?" Tears rolled down Evan's cheeks.

Raven put a hand on Evan's shoulder. "Gunnar was followin' my lead. It was necessary."

"I… don't understand. I never thought I'd see you again."

"I knew the Destroyer would get captured with a Federation giving Archer inside info. The Marauders wanted to get at me since takin' in their last leader twenty years ago. Getting' their hands on that big of a ship was somethin' I knew they couldn't pass up. And I knew I could use it to lead me right to the whole lot of 'em."

"How did you survive the attack? I saw the ship fall into a black hole."

"Escape pod. I slipped through a sub space envelope and went into hiding. Been out here ever since. I've monitored the Destroyer the whole time. Every transmission in an' outta that hunk of junk was routed right out here to the Leviathan."

Evan hugged his father again. "I'm so glad you're all right."

"Say…" Raven looked his son over. "Where's all your gadgets?"

"Archer roughed us up a little," Gunnar said.

"You guys okay?" Raven looked more concerned about Evan, holding his face between his hands.

"Now that I know you're alive, everything's perfect."

"There's no limit to Archer's cruelty. Or greed. We better jump back over to Fomalhaut. Gimme the Core Chips and we'll fire this big boy up."

"They were lost with the Frigate," Gunnar said, looking at Evan.

Raven studied his son. Evan drew in a breath, face flushed. "Haven't I told you a million times--"

"Wait, wait," Evan said reaching back into his plasti-skin vest compartment. "They weren't destroyed."

"Archer said--"

"I lied." Evan pulled the chips out, holding them out to his dad. He grinned. "'Captain's rule number one. Never leave without the Core Chips.' I'd never let anyone get them."

Raven smiled. "That's my boy." He clapped the side of Evan's shoulder. He put the chips into slots at the edge of the control panel. "Now let's get going. We got a traitor to catch."

"The Feds are already there," Gunnar said. "That's how we got away. McMurrary's takin' care of the Marauders and rescuin' the slaves."

Raven called up a holographic display. "Didn't you wonder why your rescue was so easy? There's somethin' you better see."

*   *   *

The Federation Cruiser floated high over an asteroid swam orbiting Fomalhaut. On the bridge, Admiral McMurrary studied a holographic projection of the Eusian Dreadnaught. "It appears the Empire has been involved in a lot of covert technological developments lately," he said. He turned to Bolton Archer. "Dreadnaught could be disastrous to Federation and Marauder interests."

"I've been sayin' for years, you can't trust those Eusian reptiles. The minute you turn your back on them, they'll snap their jaws on you. Just like a swamp gator."

Exaggerated claim, given his criminal record.

"How do you think I lost this eye?" Bolton pointed to the plate covering his right socket. "They're sneaky and underhanded. The only thing they're good for is a nice set of luggage."

"A lot of Federation people share you sentiments."

"Good thing we're already allies."

McMurrary nodded. "Did you get the cloak installed on the Destroyer?"

"My techs are workin' on it. There's a short in the system or something. You hit us pretty hard to spring those guys."

"You knew the plan. We had to make it look real. Now that they're not breathing down our necks, we can take your scheme to the next level."

Archer grinned, placing a gloved hand on the Admiral's shoulder. "I think the job's gonna be a whole lot easier now." He pointed at the hologram of the Dreadnaught. "Imagine the kind of empire we can build conquering worlds with that." Bolton slapped McMurrary's back, smiling wide as he stared at the schematic.

The Admiral smiled. "Where's the Dreadnaught located?"

"HR 7578. Completely unarmed. It doesn't have any blood diamonds to focus plasma. Yet. We'll bring 'em ourselves. I've stepped up the search. My slaves are working round the clock. I'll break every one of their lizard backs if I have to."

Archer slowly walked over to the view port, hands behind him. "I heard you wanted to retire soon."

"That's right."

"Just think of the pension plan you'll have now, Admiral. No planet will be able to stand up to us. We can topple every government in the Federation and beyond."

"I always knew you were ambitious," McMurrary said. "No wonder the F.F.P. couldn't keep you in its ranks."

"I didn't get where I am by being soft." He circled McMurrary. "Don't look so glum, Admiral. I'm about to make you a very wealthy man." He pinched the Admiral's left cheek. "All we have to do is cloak the Destroyer, dock with Dreadnaught, and infiltrate it."

*   *   *

The immense Leviathan jumped into the Fomalhaut system. "Shields," Raven said. "Charge all weapons. It won't taken 'em long to spot a ship this big." He threw a quick look over to Gunnar. "When can we expect Kolt's forces?"

"Any minute."

"Get detailed scans of the system, Evan. We wanna be able to tell Kolt's guys right where to go to find the slaves."

"Aye, dad."

"The stakes have been raised," Gunnar said.

"How so?"

"The Eusians built something called a Dreadnaught. Archer wants it. Bad."

Raven stared at the debris swarm ahead. "That means he'll need a whole bunch of diamonds. See any out there, Medium Fries?"

Evan skimmed holographic data. "One asteroid with a good deposit. Not big enough for a mining camp."

"Do they got it?"

"No."

"Maybe we can create a diversion until Kolt gets here." Raven sighed. "Time to go out and earn that Pilot's license."

"Dad?"

"Get down to the main hanger. I want you to take your 'Vette out and tractor that stone right into the sun. We'll watch your tail from here."

Evan blinked his eyes and snapped his head. "Okay. I'm on it." He ran toward the turbo lift.

"Don't get your butt blown off out there."

A holographic light flashed and an alarm sounded. "They've spotted us," Gunnar said.

"Time to kick this party into high gear."

*   *   *

The holographic star system map clearly pinpointed the Leviathan. Archer smiled. He swung his head to Admiral McMurrary. "I think we can beef up our fleet. Don't you?" He pressed a button, activating a communication screen. The face of one of his fellow Marauders appeared. "Get a squad out there an' capture me a Leviathan."

*   *   *

Matching the asteroid's orbital velocity, Evan slid up along side the massive chunk of space debris. He engaged the tractor beam and gently tugged the boulder into a new orbit. "Got it," he said. He accelerated toward Fomalhaut.

*   *   *

"What's this one doin' here?" Archer asked, studying the holographic display. A second, smaller ship was towing an asteroid toward the star. "Something's not right." He pulled up another screen, scanning the rock. "It's full of blood diamonds. What the hell does he think he's doin'…?"

Bolton switched back to his communication screen. "Send someone out after the second ship and retrieve that asteroid."

*   *   *

"Swoop Jets comin' in," Gunnar said.

"Let 'em have it."

Gunnar touched a series of buttons. Polaron Cannon turrets spat yellow beams of energy from all defensive points along the length of the Leviathan. Rail gun pellets formed a wild, cris-crossing maelstrom. Missiles screamed into the void. All around the hull, small metal canisters floated into space.

"This bad boy came packed!"

"You know me, Gunnar. I've been salvagin' parts from shipyards for years."

The Swoop Jets changed course to avoid the Polaron bursts. A few got caught up in rail gun flack, spinning wildly away. Two others tried to out maneuver missiles and ended up cooked. Three Jets came too close to the colossal bulk of the Leviathan and flew right into the swarm of space mines and exploded.

*   *   *

Focused on towing the asteroid toward the sun, Evan jumped when an alarm sounded in the cockpit. A hologram popped up, warning him that Swoop Jets were approaching. "Guys, I got company."

"Go to maximum, kid," Gunnar's voice said.

Evan pushed the wheel in gradually, careful not to loose his grip on the rock. He smiled when he saw the Swoop Jets couldn't keep up.

*   *   *

"Sir, the Leviathan's armed to the hilt. We're not gonna be able to take it with fighters."

Archer spun to McMurrary. "Who the hell ever heard of an armed Leviathan? These guys aren't prospectors, that's for certain." He rotated back to the screen. "What about that little runt towing my diamonds into the star?" His head tilted in McMurrary's direction.

"Too fast for us. He's in a modified Racing 'Vette."

McMurrary's eyes opened wide. "What do you know?" Bolton asked.

"Gunnar Spade and the kid were in a Racing Corvette."

Archer leaned on the counsel, glaring at controls rather than the holographic projection. "So, they're out there tyrin' to make trouble, are they?" He lifted his head to the communications screen. "Get the Destroyer out of the docking area and ready the Gunboat." He leered at the Admiral. "We're gonna hunt us a Leviathan."

*   *   *

Sensors in Evan's cockpit flashed. He deactivated the tractor beam. The asteroid tumbled along its intended trajectory and disappeared in the glare of Fomalhaut's photosphere. "Mission accomplished on my end," Evan said.

"Good work," Raven acknowledged.

*   *   *

"Looks like Archer's playin' for keeps," Gunnar said. "We got a Destroyer, a Gunboat, and the Cruiser bearing down on us."

"How you doin' out there, Evan?"

"Just docked."

"Good to know."

"The Cruiser's signaling."

Raven shrugged. "We've got nothin' to loose."

Gunnar nodded. He pressed a button. A holographic communications screen appeared before them. Bolton Archer and Admiral McMurrary stood next to each other. "Come back for more hospitality, Spade?" Archer asked. His eyes drifted over to Raven and the anger melted from his face. McMurrary was visibly shaken. "No. It can't be," Bolton said.

Evan ran out of the turbo lift, taking his place next to his father. "Back from the dead," Raven said. "You ever hear that old sayin' about what comes around goes around? It's your time to go, so, I'm around." Raven's eyes narrowed. "Good to see I knew you so well, Admiral. Never pegged you for a traitor. What was your price? I don't wanna know. That's what greed does to a man, right?""

"The Federation Fleet just jumped into the system," Gunnar said.

"What Federation Fleet?" McMurrary asked. He stepped out of sight, but, his voice was still picked up by the receiver. "There's not supposed to be any other ships in this area. Find out who it is."

"There's a swarm of Federation Fighters inbound to our primary targets," Gunnar said.

Bolton's head cocked sideways. "Shit," he spat.

"That's right, Marauder slime. We're droppin' the hammer on ya. You won't get away this time," Raven said.

"Kolt's signaling," Evan said. Archer leaned close to the holographic projection.

"Put him through."

"Captain Spade. I'm glad to see the reports of your death were inaccurate."

"Thank you, Lieutenant General."

Archer twisted around to McMurrary. "I thought you said you could trust him."

"Kolt, we're gonna send you scans of the asteroid swam. You're gonna see there're a lot of artificial caverns. These are Bolton Archer's infamous prison camps." Bolton's eyes grew wide as he listened. "There's a lot of Eusians out there who're gonna be real happy to see you."

"Incoming!" someone on the Cruiser bridge yelled.

Archer turned away from the communications system. He barked unintelligible orders. Then he turned to McMurrary. "Make the jump to HR 7578!" He stormed out of view.

"Well, now we know where to go lookin' for the Dreadnaught," Raven said. "Cut the transmission."

"Aye, dad." Evan touched a button.

"Get ready to jump. If Archer manages to get away, I want to be right on his tail."

*   *   *

Federation Fighters clustered around the small fleet of Federation issue Pirate controlled ships. They opened fire, chewing up hull plating and any available Swoop Jets that dropped from docking bays. The Cruiser changed direction, shaking some of the attackers. A multitude of large Federation warships closed up ranks around the Gunboat and Destroyer, popping shell after shell into them.

In short order, the Gunboat swelled into a fiery red cloud of gas. Precision targeting of the Destroyer's engines left if crippled. Limping forward, smoke plumes leaked from the damaged Cruiser. Like buzzing mosquitoes, the smaller fighters encircled the craft. The Leviathan followed, pelting the Cruiser with a barrage of rail gun pellets and rockets.

Fanning out across the system, most of the larger Federation ships pulled up to asteroids. "We're deploying rescue teams," Kolt told Raven.

"Signal Archer, audio only," Raven said to Gunnar.

"It's through."

"Better give up while you got the chance. You try to jump now and you'll leave a string of debris from here to--"

"He cut us off."

Raven shrugged. "Fine. Have it your way."

A white lance of energy shot out of the front of the Cruiser. It lurched forward and disappeared.

"Looks like Archer and McMurray got away," Kolt said.

"They didn't get far," Raven said. "We're goin' after 'em. "You rescue those slaves."

"Good luck, Captain Spade." Raven nodded. Kolt's image disappeared. "Let's make that jump."

*   *   *

The Dreadnaught was a truly awesome sight to behold. In comparison, its massive flared body dwarfed the Leviathan. The odd configuration of the hull plating made it appear more organic than artificially constructed.

Standing at Evan's side, Gunnar leaned down to his ear. "Now that's blutotanic."

"Got a fix on the Cruiser?" Raven asked.

"There's some kind of Scattering Field. I can't cut through it.

"Federation?"

Gunnar looked confused. "No. Eusian."

"Well, what do you know..."

"I'm reading some really strong, concentrated pockets of energy."

"Where?"

Gunnar shook his head. "Here on the bridge."

Three Eusian soldiers in green uniforms materialized on deck. Raven stood, his body tense. "I hope you're a welcoming party. Federation Intel suggested The Marauders wanted to align themselves with the Eusian Empire. I'd wager with that ship out there, they'd be unstoppable."

"We apologize for this abrupt appearance," the soldier in the middle said. "It's not in habit of the Eusian Military to use this technology as intrusive. The Eusian Matriarch deployed us here. We need your help to stop the pirates. Project Dreadnaught has no plasma focusing diamonds. We must ask if you have."

"I'm sorry, we don't," Raven said.

The Eusian lowered his head, shaking it from side-to-side. "Only one diamond is needed."

Evan's eyes lit up. "Wait." He pulled the necklace presented to him by Viceroy Wexam from under his plasti-skin vest. "I have one. Will this work?" Evan held it out.

"Yes, it will." The Eusian came over to take it, bowing deeply. "We're greatly indebted to you." He resumed standing between his companions. "We must warn you to keep a safe distance." In an instant, they vanished.

"Zoom in, Gunnar. Let's watch the show."

Gunnar smirked, pulling up a holographic projection. The tracking computer took a few moments before it located the Cruiser and then locked on its energy signature. The view enlarged, providing them with a perfect view.

A reddish discharge from the nose of the Dreadnaught exploded a few tens of meters away from the Cruiser's bridge. The ball of expanding gas pulled back on itself, crushing down into an infinitely dense point. The Cruiser shifted it center of mass, tilting sideways toward the singularity. Its engines fired, holding the ship back from the swirling blue event horizon, but it continued to tip. Tritanium hull stretched and buckled. Fragments were sucked instantly into he gaping maw of the mini black hole. Gun turrets and communication towers were ripped apart. A few escape pods launched. They were effortlessly pulled and dragged down. Reaching a forty-five degree angle list, the bridge section of the ship split apart like an exploding tree trunk. The exhaust ports stopped glowing and power failed.

The once mighty Federation Cruiser crumbled, falling into the hole. A millisecond later, the singularity sealed itself and vanished.

Evan, Gunnar, and Raven all sat on the bridge in total silence, attention fixed on the display for long moments. Gunnar eventually deactivated it. "After all this time…" Raven said. "They're finally gone."

The Eusian soldiers materialized on the Leviathan's bridge once again. There were also many others, some holding spears with axe-blade tips. Raven stood straight. Evan's heart thumped in his chest. He stayed close to his father. Gunnar kept a close watch on them. "So this is it?" Raven asked. "You finish them off an' then take over the operation for yourselves?"

The Eusian Matriarch smiled warmly, slowly walking toward the trio of humans. "You misunderstand our intentions. I am the Eusian Matriarch. I came here to thank you for helping free my people. You will be most revered."

They blew out tensely held breaths and smiled. "I would also like to meet with top Federation Of Free Planets Officials. I came to hire you…" she pointed at Raven's chest, "…for safe passage into Federation territory."

Raven laughed heartily. He extended his hand to the Eusian Matriarch and gently held her leathery palm. "Welcome aboard, your majesty."

One of the soldiers walked up to her side and bowed before Raven and Evan. He gave the diamond necklace back to the youngster and shook his hand.

*   *   *

"You will soon be presented," Viceroy Wexam said as he poked his head back in from the dark blue velvet drapes.

Raven, Evan, and Gunnar were all out of their element dressed in suits. As he fixed his sleeves, Raven noticed Evan had his sneakers on. He laughed and tussled Evan's unruly hair. "You goofy kid," he said.

Gunnar fumbled with his tie. "What'd he do now?"

"Only my little Raptor would wear sneakers with a suit." Evan pulled his necklace out so the red stone rested on his black tie.

"You look fine, young man," Wexam said, helping with Gunnar's knot. "Only a formality this is."

"What are we gonna do after this, dad?"

"Got a surprise for ya."

Evan rolled his eyes. "Oh great."

"Been a lot of those lately, right Evan?" Gunnar nudged his arm.

"It's a good one, Medium Fries," Raven said. He lowered himself on his knees. "There's a whole part of our family you're going to get to meet."

"Oh yeah? Who?"

Raven shrugged. "How 'bout you mom, for starters."

"My mom's alive?

"And your sister."

"I have a sister, too?" Evan took a second to absorb the information. "This is so cool."

"Lillian Randolph, your mom, and Tash have been waiting for me to clear this whole mess up."

"Where?"

"On Marineau."

"You're joking, right?

"Nope," Raven shook his head.

"Tash like to pull guys' arms out of their sockets?"

"That's what 'er mom says."

"I can't believe this. I met Tash the last time we were there."

"Really?" Raven stood his full height. "You two got along okay?"

"Yeah," Evan nodded.

"Good. Then she won't have to twist your arms off."

"It is time," the Viceroy said. "Out you go now." He led Raven to the drape by his arm and held it aside with his wooden scepter.

Presidents, royalty, and dignitaries from all corners of the known galaxy filled the amphitheater. They stood, applauding loudly for several minutes. Embarrassed, the three blushed and raised their hands in greeting.

The Eusian Matriarch walked over to them and led them to the central part of the stage. Evan noticed a building sized holographic projection of the ceremony hovering in the air over their heads. The Eusian Matriarch motioned them to stand near the microphone. She smiled at the crowd, raising her hands. The applause slowly stopped.

"It is with the greatest of honor that I thank Raven Spade, Evan Spade, and Gunnar Spade, not only for their assistance in bringing an end to The Marauders' reign of terror, but also for helping free my people from the brutal episode of bondage so many Federations thought would bring war between our peoples. I give my word, their rewards shall be great." Another round of applause carried over from the crowd.

"But, more importantly, we intend to greet the bright new future between the Federation and the Eusian Empire by bestowing upon the family Spade the highest honor one species can to another. Henceforth, they are granted official citizenship of the Eusian Empire with all rights and privileges that entails." There was more applause. A round of bows and thank yous were exchanged between the Eusian Matriarch and the Spades.

"And finally, after so many long years of remaining in isolation from the galaxy, it is the wish of my people to open our borders to free trade with every planet of the Federation." The entire audience stood. Thunderous applause filled the amphitheater.

Printed by Books on Demand GmbH, Norderstedt / Germany